THE SLEEPING LADY

RETOLD BY
ANN DIXON

PAINTINGS BY
ELIZABETH JOHNS

Alaska Northwest Books™
ANCHORAGE • SEATTLE • PORTLAND

To peacemakers, present and future

ACKNOWLEDGMENTS

This book is written with thanks to James Fall and James Kari,
for their information on the origins of the story;
and to Nancy Lesh, for her help and encouragement.
With gratitude and respect, I honor the memories of
Mildred Jacobsson, for her work in preserving the story,
and Shem Pete, for sharing his knowledge of local Dena'ina culture.

Library of Congress Catalog Card number 94-9157
ISBN 0-88240-444-X

Managing Editor: Ellen Wheat
Editor: Carolyn Smith
Cover and Book Designer: Judythe Sieck

The paintings in this book are in oil on canvas.
The display type is Kabel Medium.
The text type is Maximal Medium.
Calligraphy by Judythe Sieck
Composition by Ultratype & Graphics, San Diego, California
Printed on Kashmir acid-free paper

Alaska Northwest Books™
An imprint of Graphic Arts Center Publishing Company
Editorial office: 2208 NW Market Street, Suite 300, Seattle, WA 98107
Catalog and order dept.: P.O. Box 10306, Portland, OR 97210
800-452-3032

Printed in the United States of America

A NOTE TO THE READER

Mount Susitna, popularly known in Southcentral Alaska as ''The Sleeping Lady,'' lies across Cook Inlet from the city of Anchorage. Through the years, the story of the mountain of the Sleeping Lady has traveled by word of mouth, though the origin of the story is unknown. It may have begun with homesteaders or prospectors in Southcentral Alaska, perhaps between the 1930s and 1950s. The earliest published version I have found was written for a regional magazine in 1966 by Nancy Lesh, now an Anchorage librarian. In the 1970s, at least two other versions appeared in print, one by Mildred Jacobsson and another by Olive Joslin Bell.

Many people believe that the legend of the Sleeping Lady is Native Alaskan in origin. While ''Susitna'' is an Athabascan word, the story is not a Native legend, according to Shem Pete, the now-deceased Dena'ina elder who spent much of his later life documenting Dena'ina culture and legends, as well as James Kari, of the Alaska Native Language Center at the University of Alaska-Fairbanks, and James Fall, of the Alaska Department of Fish and Game.

Once, long ago in Alaska, there lived a race of giant people along the shores of Cook Inlet.

The land then was warm and covered with fruit trees of every kind.

Woolly mammoths and saber-toothed tigers roamed the forests and beaches but did not harm the gentle Inlet people.

Peace and happiness ruled the land.

Especially happy were a young man named Nekatla and a young woman named Susitna, for they were in love and soon to be married.

As the wedding day neared, the Inlet people eagerly prepared for the celebration.

But the day before the wedding a stranger burst into the village.

"Danger!" he cried. "Warriors from the north are coming! They roam from village to village, killing people, stealing from them, and burning their homes!"

"Stranger, how do you know this?" someone asked.

The man's face clouded with pain.

"They have destroyed my village, my family. . . everything," he answered. "Only I escaped. Beware, these people are cruel and crazed for blood!"

All plans for the wedding were forgotten.

The villagers gathered in council.

First one person spoke, then another. Some thought they should quickly fashion weapons and attack the warriors. Others thought they should prepare to fight the warriors when they came to the village. Still others wanted to hide in the forest until the warriors passed them by.

Nekatla and Susitna listened in silence, their hearts deeply troubled.

After everyone had spoken, Nekatla rose.

"I, too, have an idea," he began. "But I do not know if there are people here brave enough to go with me. I say this: I will not fight these people and neither should you. We have few weapons, for we gave up the ways of war long ago. We've learned a better way, which is peace."

Many of the people nodded their heads in agreement.

"Continue," the elders encouraged him.

"I will not run away from this danger, for then the warriors will kill many more. This is my proposal: we travel north to meet them. We convince them to lay down their weapons and live in peace. We will carry gifts rather than weapons so they'll have no reason to attack us.

"And I am willing to go first."

It was a bold plan but the people agreed to it. All the men of the village would go.

Immediately everyone began preparing for the dangerous journey north.

By morning the men were ready to leave.

Sadly, Susitna and Nekatla said goodbye on a hill above the village where they had spent many hours together.

"We will be married as soon as I return," promised Nekatla.

"I will wait for you at this very spot," answered Susitna.

Susitna watched thoughtfully, hopefully, until the forms of the men disappeared into the forested mountains.

Susitna made ready to wait. She ran back to the village for her needles, knife, and baskets, then busied herself gathering nuts and berries.

On the second day she tired of gathering fruit, so she cut roots and grasses to weave into baskets. This task amused her for many hours, but eventually she tired of making baskets, too.

Susitna spent the third day sewing, for she was too weary to gather fruit and cut grasses. Yet she could not sleep, wondering if the men had succeeded in their mission.

Perhaps Nekatla would return at any moment!

But many days and nights went by, each more slowly than the last. Finally Susitna could no longer pick berries, weave baskets, or even sew.

"I will lie down just for a moment," she said finally.

And she fell fast asleep.

While Susitna slept, word of a terrible battle reached her village.

"Nekatla was brave," reported a boy who had escaped. "He led our men to meet with the warriors. But as he and their leader were about to speak, someone threw a spear! Their men set upon ours and we fought until all our men were dead or dying, and many of theirs, too."

The women and children wept to hear the names of the fathers, sons, and brothers they had lost.

When the women went to tell Susitna the terrible news, they couldn't bear to wake her from such peaceful sleep.

Let her rest, they decided. *Why break her heart any sooner than we must?*

And they wove a blanket of soft grasses and wildflower blossoms, which they gently laid over her.

May Susitna always dream of her lover, they prayed.

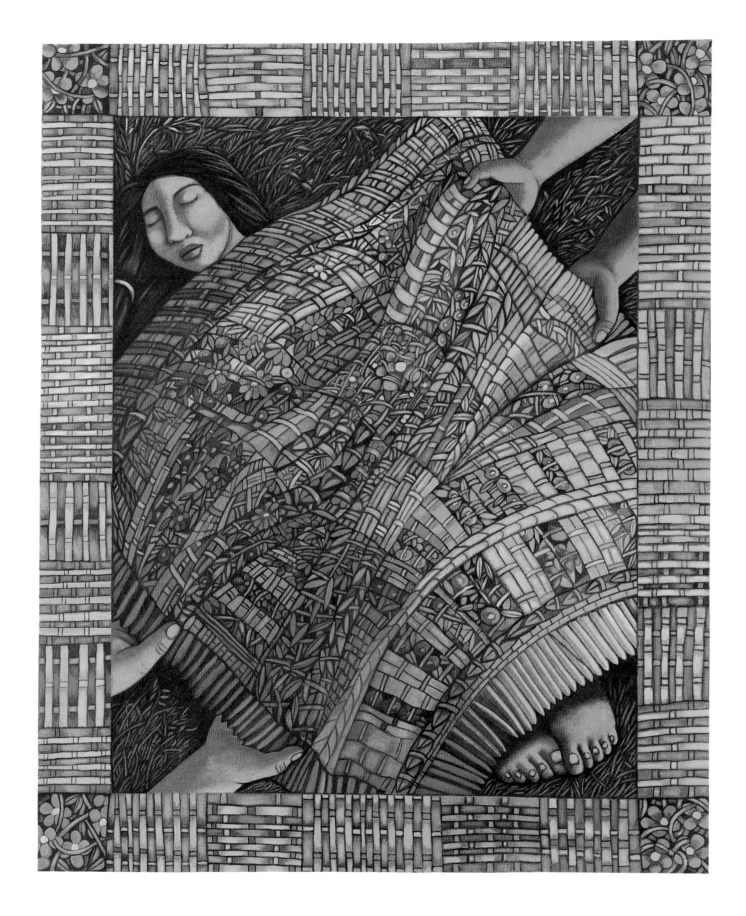

That night all warmth and joy left the village. As the air grew colder and colder, Susitna settled more deeply into sleep.

All around her, the fruit trees froze and died, falling like the men in battle.

The tears of the villagers gathered into clouds and, in the chill air, returned to earth as Alaska's first snowfall.

The snow fell slowly at first, one flake at a time, but soon it filled the sky, spreading thickly across the entire land.

For seven days and nights the snow fell, until Susitna and all her people lay beneath a blanket of shimmering white.

Days passed into years, and years into hundreds and thousands of years.

For a few months each summer, warmth returned to the land, allowing birch trees and spruce and willow to grow.

Grizzly bears, moose, and other new animals appeared, taking the place of the old.

After a long time a new race of humans, smaller than the first, came to stay.

Today Susitna still sleeps through the seasons, dreaming of Nekatla.

If you look across Cook Inlet in the winter, you can see her covered by a snowy quilt.

In summer, you see her resting beneath a green and flowered blanket.

It is said that when the people of war change their ways and peace rules the earth, Nekatla will return.

Then Susitna, the Sleeping Lady, will awake.